For Prince Husband – JG

For the innate abilities that
want to come forward in all
princesses and princes – LH

A special thanks to Marlo Garnsworthy,
the picture book whisperer.

Published in the United States of America

NY Media Works, LLC

TriBeCa, NYC

For ordering information contact BubblegumPrincess@nymediaworks.com

Educators and Librarians, for a teacher's guide, visit www.nymediaworks.com/Books.html

Visit us on the Web! www.nymediaworks.com

Publisher's Cataloging-in-Publication

Gribble, Julie.

Bubblegum Princess / by Julie Gribble ; illustrations by Lori Hanson. –1st ed.

p. cm.

Summary: Katy delights in blowing bubblegum bubbles, a decidedly unladylike habit.
Despite opposition, she teaches the kingdom to love bubblegum bubbles as much as she does.

ISBN-13: 978-0-9890914-0-4   (hardcover)

ISBN-13: 978-0-9890914-1-1   (eBook)

[1. Princesses–Fiction. 2. Princes–Fiction. 3. Bubble gum–Fiction.   4. Etiquette–Fiction.]

I. Hanson, Lori, ill. II. Title.

PZ8.G8555Bub 2013

[E] QBI13-600079

2013908274

Printed in China

First Edition

10 9 8 7 6 5 4 3 2 1

Bubblegum Princess

by Julie Gribble
illustrations by Lori Hanson

NY Media Works · New York

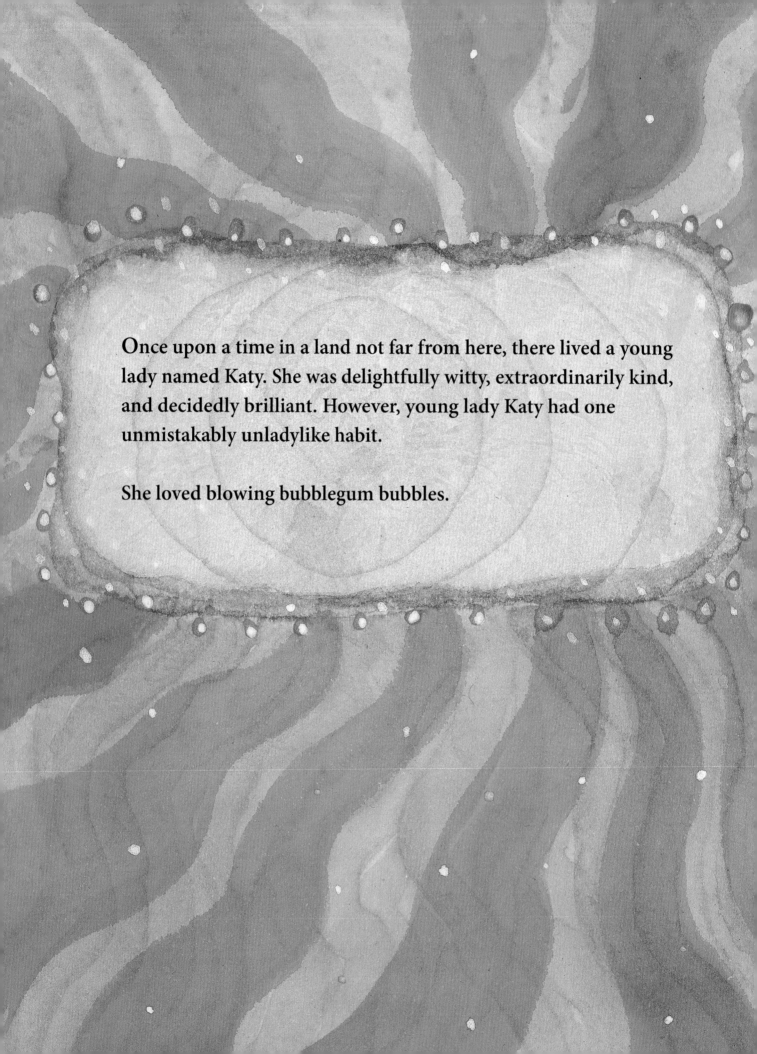

Once upon a time in a land not far from here, there lived a young lady named Katy. She was delightfully witty, extraordinarily kind, and decidedly brilliant. However, young lady Katy had one unmistakably unladylike habit.

She loved blowing bubblegum bubbles.

"Singularly silly," said Mum.
"Utterly disgraceful," said Dad.
"Stupendously bad," they agreed.

Katy would blow bubbles while biking,
blow bubbles while baking,
blow bubbles when
bouncing to bed.

She'd blow bubbles at sunup, at noontime, and naptime.
No one fancied bubbles more than she did.

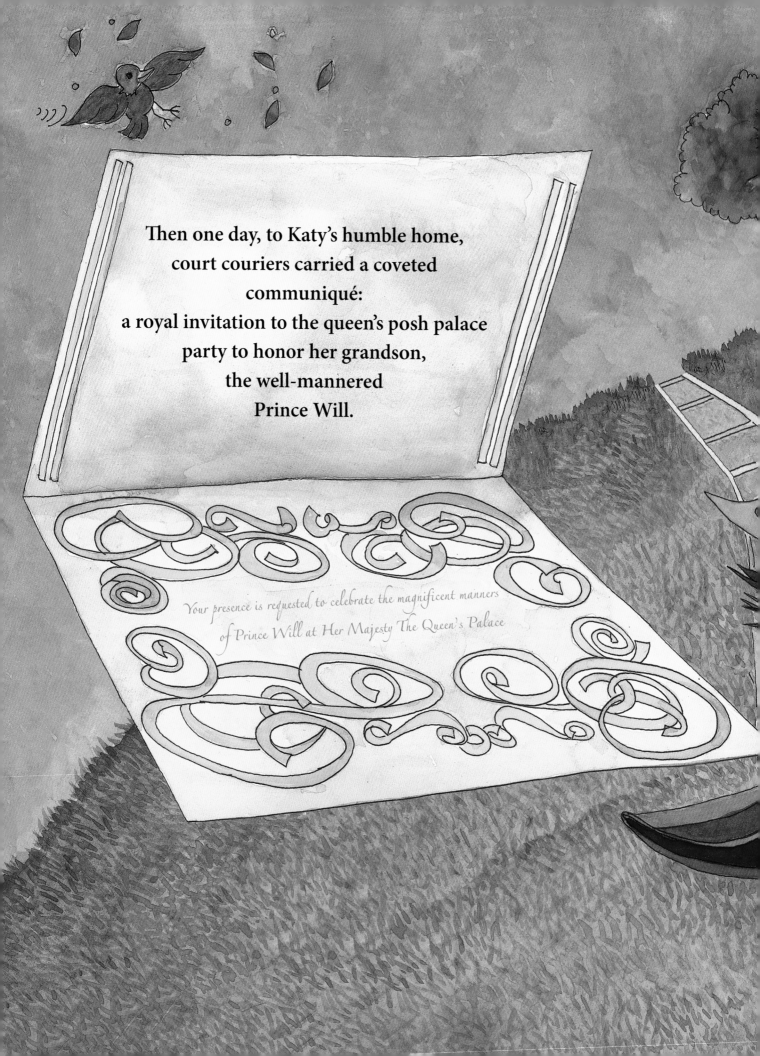

Then one day, to Katy's humble home,
court couriers carried a coveted
communiqué:
a royal invitation to the queen's posh palace
party to honor her grandson,
the well-mannered
Prince Will.

*Your presence is requested to celebrate the magnificent manners
of Prince Will at Her Majesty The Queen's Palace*

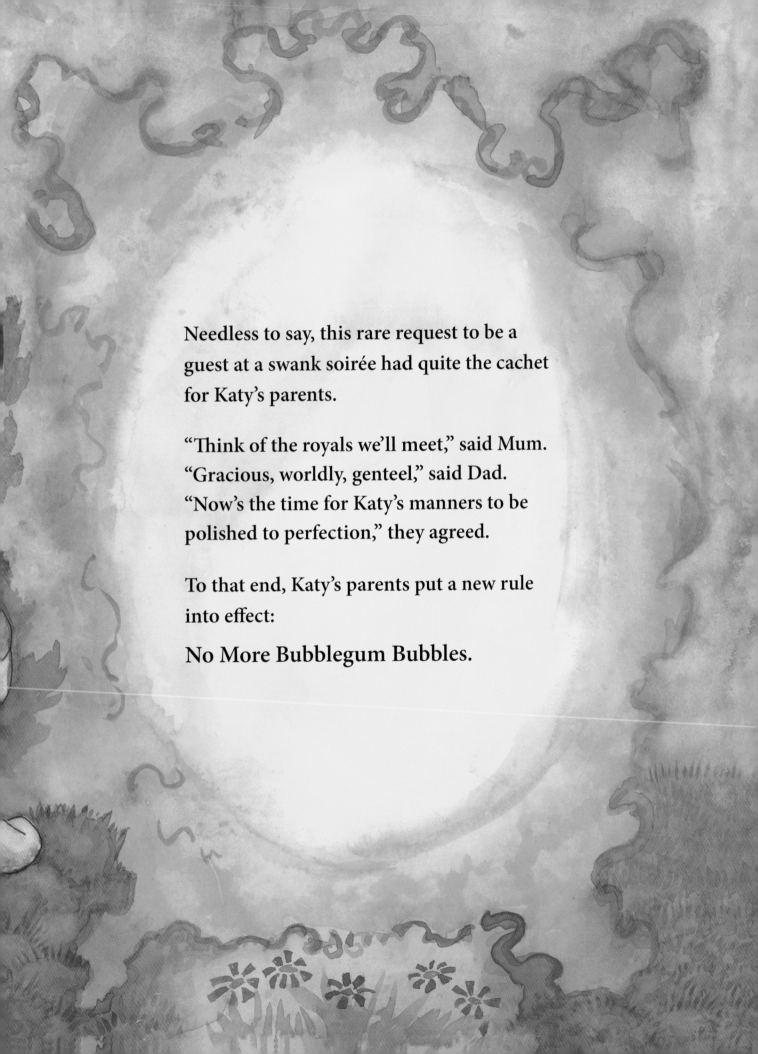

Needless to say, this rare request to be a guest at a swank soirée had quite the cachet for Katy's parents.

"Think of the royals we'll meet," said Mum. "Gracious, worldly, genteel," said Dad. "Now's the time for Katy's manners to be polished to perfection," they agreed.

To that end, Katy's parents put a new rule into effect:

No More Bubblegum Bubbles.

"How unfair," said Katy. "Big, Brobdingnagian bubbles are my triumph, my joy. I could not care less about meeting a prince!"

But Katy quit blowing bubbles then and there, on the spot.

And all at once, life without gum became gloomy and glum.

Soon the day arrived for young lady Katy and her family to attend the queen's soirée.

Mum wore her best dress, and Dad sported his finest bow tie.

Katy carried her prettiest purse, and just to be safe, she gave her secret stash of gum to her mum.

At the palace party, Katy remained on her best no-bubble behavior, an exemplar of decorum, gracious and polite, not one bubblegum bubble in sight.

But, as soon as the queen arrived, a big bubblegum bubble appeared.

It billowed
and jounced,
bobbed and
bounced, until...

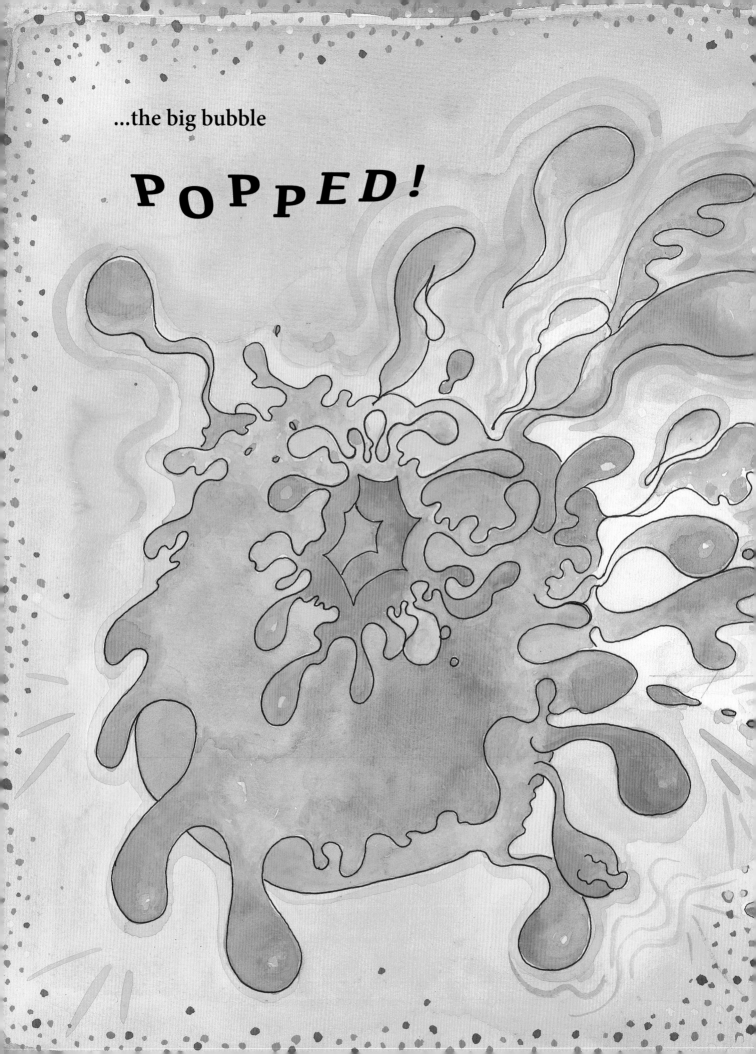

...the big bubble

PoPpED!

And there stood Katy, mid-curtsy, covered in bubblegum goo from her head to her shiny new shoes. And even her pretty purse, too.

The royals burst out laughing. The queen's corgis giggled. Mum and Dad turned ruby red, doubly troubled by the big blown bubble.

But Katy was tickled pink. "That's the most magnificent bubblegum bubble I've ever seen. It must have been twice the size of the queen!"

The queen, however,
was not amused
—they seldom are—
and she promptly
banished lady Katy
from the kingdom.

Clearly, the queen is blowing the situation out of proportion," said Katy, as she and her family were escorted from the palace.

"Katy, we must now leave our home because of that bubble you blew!" said Dad.
"And any chance to meet a well-mannered prince was blown, too," said Mum.
I didn't have any bubblegum," said Katy, "but I'll find out where that bubble came from."

Katy darted back to the palace. She dodged past party guests chatting in the garden, and back through the courtyard gate. But just before Katy dashed past the prince, she noticed something odd.

"Prince Will, is that gum on your shoe?"

"I confess, I caused this bubble trouble,"
said the prince, "but, how might I
make this right, if the queen
will not forgive this slight?"

"Truly, this is all quite ridiculous," said Katy. "This kingdom needs more bubbles, not less."

So she grabbed the gum she'd given to Mum, and blew bubbles for fun as she'd always done.

The prince, all the queen's guests, and all the queen's corgis couldn't help but join in. When the giggly bubble blowing got going, a gust of wind whisked the biggest bubbles way up into the sky.

And from high above, the kingdom seemed like quite a big place with plenty of space for bubblegum bubbles.

The queen couldn't very well banish the prince, her guests, and her kin from the kingdom —nor could she kick out the corgis.

So, quick as a snap, the queen declared,

"Bubblegum bubbles are not The-Worst-Things-in-the-World."

The corgis were overjoyed.

Mum and Dad were much relieved. "Bubblegum bubble blowing is a perfect, princessly pursuit," they promptly agreed.

And Katy was happy once again.

Over the years, like the bubbles they blew, Katy and Will's bubblegum friendship grew and grew. And as patron of The Bounding Bobbling Billowing Bouncing Bubblegum Bubble Academy, Katy taught all the children in the kingdom that...

...the world is a much happier place with bubblegum bubbles in it.

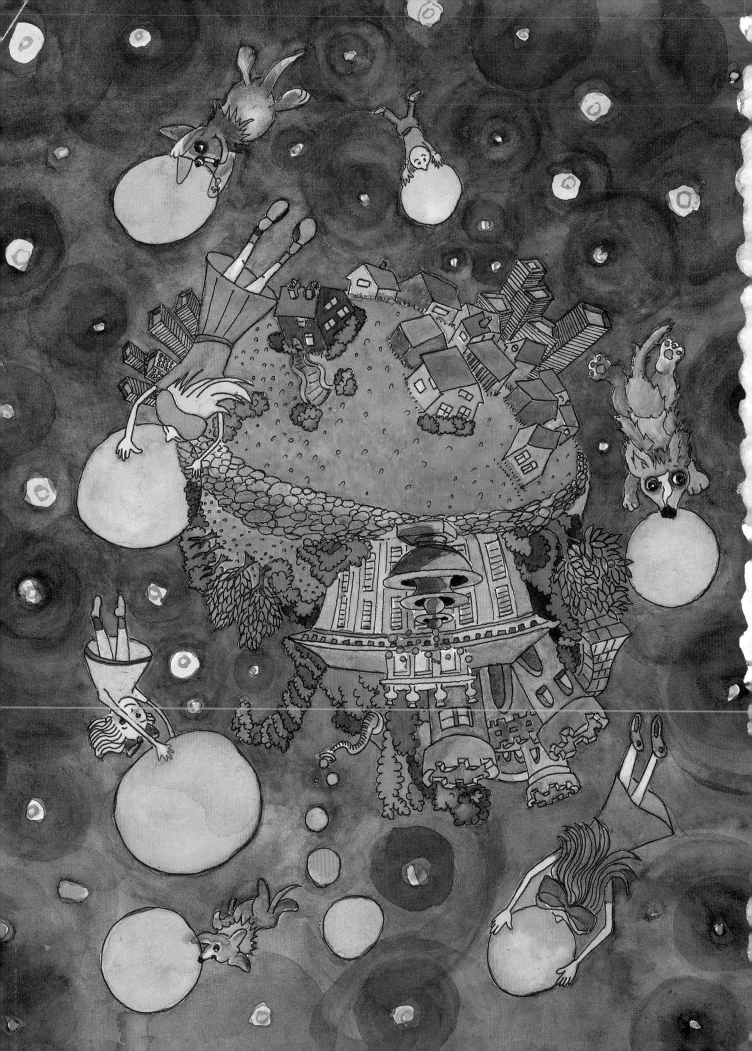